Little *Angel

Geraldine McCaughrean

*

Ian Beck

BARNES
&NOBLE
BOOKS
NEW YORK

For Susannah & Andrew Humphreys
G. McC.

For Lily
I. B.

Text copyright © 1995 by Geraldine McCaughrean
Illustrations copyright © by Ian Beck

This edition published by Barnes & Noble, Inc.,
by arrangement with Orchard Books, a division of Watts Publishing Group.

1998 Barnes & Noble Books

ISBN 0-7607-1125-9

Printed in Hong Kong

98 99 00 01 02 M 9 8 7 6 5 4 3 2 1

Midas

The night was so cold, full of snowflake stars.
It was Micah's turn to keep watch over
the sheep, while the other shepherds slept.

Suddenly the air was full of singing and the sky
blizzard-white with angels.
"Don't be afraid!" cried the Archangel. "Wonderful news! A
baby was born tonight called Jesus – a king to save the world!

He's in a stable, in Bethlehem! Go and see!"
Then upwards soared the angels. Their singing grew
softer, and they were gone.

"We must see this baby! Now! Tonight!"
the shepherds exclaimed. "Micah, you stay here.
Someone must stay with the sheep."

"Oh, but…" Too late. They were already
singing their way across the fields into the dark.

Micah was afraid. "What if a wolf comes?"
he whispered.

Somewhere a sheep bleated in the dark. Or did it?
The cry came again. Micah strained his ears to hear.
"Help! Help!" It was not very far away.
A little angel hung upside down in a tree,
her wings in tatters.

"I got caught up," she said. "The others went back to watch over Jesus. I called out for help, but they were singing too loud. They went without me!"

Micah helped her down. "I was left behind too," he said. "Have you seen him? The little king?"

"Oh yes! He was wonderful! Marvelous! I can't describe… But I must catch them up! In the morning they will leave for the Country of Angels and I may never get home! Only the Archangel can mend my wings."

"And I must get back to my flock," said Micah.

"What flock?" asked the little angel.

But for two old ewes,
there was not a sheep to be seen.

"A wolf must have come by and scattered them,"
Micah wailed. "I must find them! I was left in charge!"

"I'll help you look," said the little angel. "Angels are
supposed to help people."

"No, no. You must catch up with the other angels," said Micah. "Get your wings mended. Go quickly. I'll manage."

The shepherd boy watched her go. First she stepped into a rabbit hole. Then she tripped over a root. Next she went sprawling into a ditch. Then she sank deep into a bog.

"I think I had better take you there," said Micah,
helping her out. "You might meet a wolf on the way."

"It must be wonderful to be a shepherd," said the little angel. "Oh, but to run messages for God!" said Micah. "To fly in among the planets and stars! That would be so fine!"

"For someone who liked high places, I suppose,"
the little angel said. "But I'm afraid of flying."

The shepherd boy held her hand. "It's wolves with me."
He had never told anyone before. "I'm terrified of wolves."

Suddenly a great grey wolf sprang into their path.
Its eyes were pale and flecked with red. Its teeth were
icicles, dripping.

The shepherd boy felt his heart shrink and his mouth run dry. He stepped in front of the little angel, fumbling for his slingshot.

But all of a sudden, the little angel leapt at the wolf.

Angel and wolf rolled across the ground —
grey fur and frayed feathers.

Micah swung his slingshot, but dared not hurl
the stone, for fear of hitting his friend.

Then the wolf was on its back...and the little
angel was laughing out loud!

The wolf too was grinning and its bushy tail thumped
the ground. The little angel was tickling the wolf!
"I like animals," she said.

And they all walked on to Bethlehem.

As they got closer to the town, they thought the streets were full of snow. Then they saw what had become of Micah's sheep.

The sheep, too, had heard the cry of the angels, and
come on a journey of their own to Bethlehem, to the stable.
"I suppose everyone wants to see the newborn king,"
said Micah.

They could hear the angels singing softly.
"Come in with me," said the little angel.
"Can't," said Micah. "The shepherds would see me.
They'd know I left the field."

"They won't see us if we creep in at the back,"
said the little angel. "And there will never be a more
marvelous sight in the history of the world!"
So Micah and the little angel crept inside the stable.

They saw the happy mother and father, saw the donkey and the ox. But best of all, they saw the baby king sleeping peacefully in a box of straw.

Micah opened his eyes wide as wide, so that he would see everything and remember it all, all of his life.

Then they crept outside to where the Archangel was waiting.

"Oh, *there* you are," whispered the Archangel. "I was worried about you. I see you met with a bit of bad luck."

"Not at all," said the little angel, as her drooping wings were mended. "The best luck in the world! I made a friend."

Micah said, "I must drive the sheep back now."

"I'll help you," said the little angel. "Wolf and I."

They joined hands for the long walk back. Suddenly Micah's feet rose gently off the ground.

"I can fly! I can fly! But how can that be?"

"A touch of the Archangel's wings?" she suggested.

"Or a gift from the baby king," he replied.

Below them, Wolf drove the sheep home over the moonlit ground.

"We should change places!" cried the little angel. "I could stay here among the animals, you go flying among the planets!"

"Yes! Because you're not afraid of wolves!" cried Micah. ". . . though, of course, neither am I any more."

"How strange!" his friend exclaimed. "I'm not afraid of flying either! But how could that be?"
"The touch of the Archangel?" he suggested.

"Or a gift from the baby king," she replied.
Towards morning, the Christmas angels flocked
back to the Country of Angels and the littlest angel
never again complained at how high they flew.

Each Christmas night after that, while the older shepherds slept and the youngest kept watch, a little angel came visiting from beyond the whirling planets.